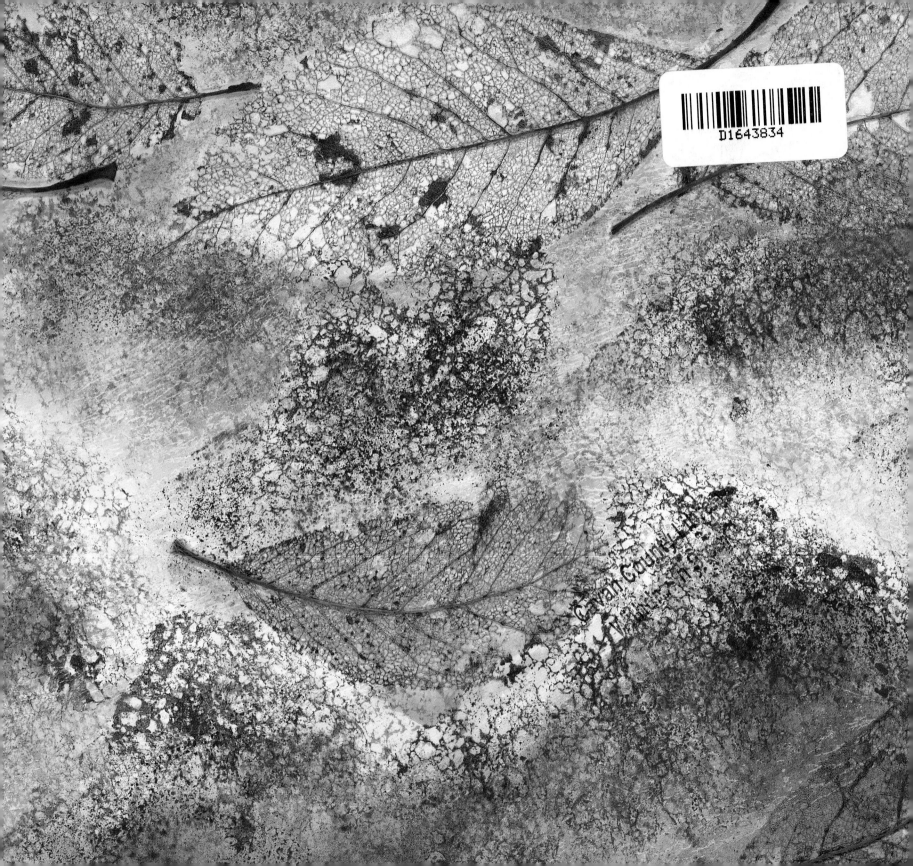

For my mother

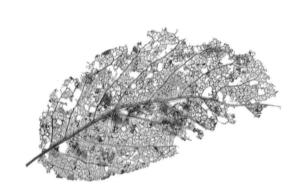

First published 2003 by Walker Books Ltd
87 Vauxhall Walk, London SE11 5HJ

10 9 8 7 6 5 4 3 2 1

© 2003 Kathy Henderson

The right of Kathy Henderson to be identified as the author and illustrator of this work has been asserted
by her in accordance with the Copyright, Designs and Patents Act 1988

This book has been typeset in Humana

Printed in Italy

British Library Cataloguing in Publication Data:
a catalogue record for this book is available from the British Library

ISBN 0-7445-8141-9

www.walkerbooks.co.uk

And The Good Brown Earth

Kathy Henderson

WALKER BOOKS
AND SUBSIDIARIES
LONDON • BOSTON • SYDNEY

When Nan went to the vegetable patch
Charlie came too.

It was nearly winter.

"Now's digging time," said Nan.
And she picked up her spade
and dug that ground
into big old lumps.

Charlie dug too.

He dug a hole and a heap

and a squashy place

for squelching in.

And the good brown earth got on with doing

what the good brown earth does best.

Next time Nan went to the vegetable patch

Charlie came too and there was snow on the ground.

Charlie ran and jumped and slid and whooped.

Nan stood and looked.

"Now's thinking time," said Nan,
thinking about all the things in her gardening book.
Charlie thought too.
He thought up a snowman.

Next time Nan went to the vegetable patch
and Charlie came too there was spring in the air.

"Now's planting time," said Nan.
And she raked out the dug earth, smooth as breadcrumbs,
and planted seeds in long, straight rows.

Charlie planted too.
Lots of seeds.
Here, there and
who knows where.

And the good brown earth got on with doing

what the good brown earth does best.

Next time Nan went to the vegetable patch Charlie came too

and the birds were singing and the trees were flowering

and the rain and the sun were chasing each other across the sky.

"Now's watching time," said Nan,

keeping an eye on those hungry birds.

And she made a scarecrow and stuck it in the ground.

Charlie watched too.

"Nan! Nan!" he shouted,

"there are green spikes coming up!"

Next time Nan and Charlie went to the vegetable patch
it was green all over.

"Now's weeding time," said Nan.

And she picked up her long-handled hoe and grubbed up
all those weed things between her vegetable rows.

Charlie pulled up a few weeds too
(at least he hoped they were weeds).
Then he rolled in the long grass and sang.

Next time Nan and Charlie went to the vegetable patch

it was hot, hot, hot.

The plants were drooping and the earth was dry.

"Uh-oh!" said Nan. "Now's watering time."

And she hooked up the hosepipe to the old tap

and ran it on the plants, sweet as rain.

Charlie watered too, mainly himself.

And he gave Nan the second ripe strawberry.

Next thing Charlie's Ma and Pa were off to the seaside
with all the family, and Nan and Charlie went too.

"Now's resting time," said Nan, stretching out for a snooze.
And the sun shone and the breeze blew…

And the good brown earth got on with doing

what the good brown earth does best,
day after golden day until...

The next time Nan went to the vegetable patch
and Charlie came too (of course),
what did they find?

"Oh wow oh wow OH WOW!"

There were Nan's plants standing tall and ripe and lush…

And there were Charlie's,

higgledy-piggledy,

tangling,
FANTASTIC!

Charlie jumped up and down
and hugged and hugged and hugged his big Nan tight.
"But what, but how, but who?" said Charlie. "All this?"

Nan hugged him back.
"You'd have to ask the good brown earth," she said.

And she took her long-pronged fork and opened up the ground
and there were pale brown potatoes like buried treasure
and carrots and parsnips and beets.

"Now's gathering time," said Nan, filling her basket.

And Charlie gathered too, beans and greens,

ladybirds and grasshoppers, dandelion clocks and fat tomatoes.

And he ate so many blackberries

that purple juice ran all down his chin.

And when they'd finished gathering

Nan and Charlie loaded up the wheelbarrow

and set off home for feasting time.

And the good brown earth got on with doing

what the good brown earth does best.

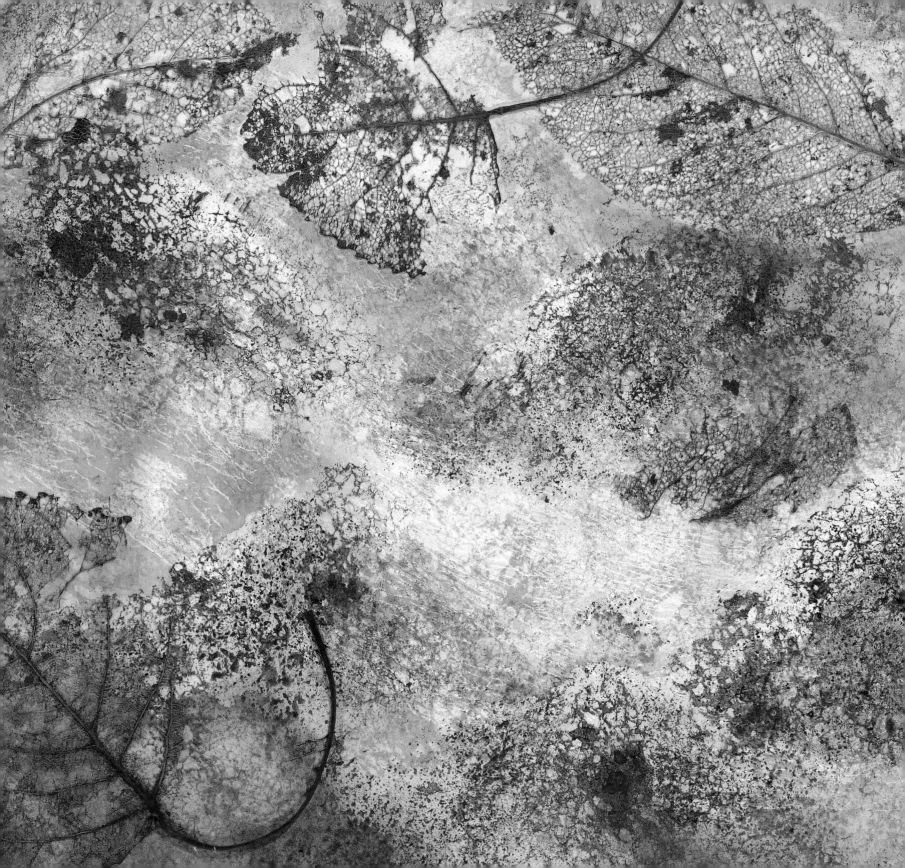